W9-AZW-449

This book belongs to:

LITTLE SIMON

An imprint of Simon & Schuster Children's Publishing Division • 1230 Avenue of the Americas, New York, New York 10020 • First Little Simon hardcover edition August 2017 • Copyright © 2017 by Simon & Schuster, Inc. All rights reserved, including the right of reproduction in whole or in part in any form. LITTLE SIMON is a registered trademark of Simon & Schuster, Inc., and associated colophon is a trademark of Simon & Schuster, Inc. For information about special discounts for bulk purchases, please contact Simon & Schuster Special Sales at 1-866-506-1949 or business@simonandschuster.com. The Simon & Schuster Speakers Bureau can bring authors to your live event. For more information or to book an event contact the Simon & Schuster Speakers Bureau at 1-866-248-3049 or visit our website at www.simonspeakers.com. Series designed by Laura Roode. Book designed by Hannah Frece. The text of this book was set in Usherwood.

Manufactured in the United States of America 0717 FFG

10 9 8 7 6 5 4 3 2 1

Cataloging-in-Publication Data is available for this title from the Library of Congress.

ISBN 978-1-4814-9436-6 (hc)
ISBN 978-1-4814-9435-9 (pbk)
ISBN 978-1-4814-9437-3 (eBook)

the adventures of

SOPHIE MOUSE

11

THE MOUSE HOUSE

By Poppy Green • Illustrated by Jennifer A. Bell

LITTLE SIMON

New York London Toronto Sydney New Delhi

Contents

～ Chapter 1 ～

A Friday Surprise

Sophie Mouse's pencil flew across her math paper. She raced to answer the bottom row of subtraction problems.

It was Friday afternoon. The whole class was taking their timed math quiz. They had to answer as many problems as they could in just five minutes.

Sophie had to work fast. But not

too fast, or she'd make mistakes.

With three problems to go, the tip of Sophie's pencil broke.

"No!" Sophie cried out. Then she clapped a hand over her mouth. There was no talking during tests.

Hattie Frog came to the rescue. From the desk next to Sophie, Hattie held out a freshly sharpened pencil. Sophie beamed at her friend.

Thank you! she mouthed noiselessly. Hattie smiled and nodded in

reply. Sophie hurried to finish the last three problems.

One done!

Two done!

Mrs. Wise stood up at her desk. Sophie scribbled the last answer just as the teacher said, "Pencils down, please. Time is up."

Sophie sat back in her seat with a sigh. At least she had finished. But Sophie wasn't sure she'd gotten them all right.

Not the best way to end the week, she thought.

As Mrs. Wise collected the papers,

there was a knock at the schoolhouse door.

"Ah-ha," Mrs. Wise said knowingly. She started toward the door. "Remember, class? I said we'd have a surprise this afternoon."

A murmur of eager anticipation filled the room. All eyes turned toward the door.

Who was there?

Mrs. Wise flung the door open wide. Standing there was a well-dressed squirrel. Sophie blinked. It was Ellie's father. And he was holding a big tray of cupcakes!

"Happy birthday, Ellie!" Mr. Squirrel called out to his daughter.

Ellie jumped up from her desk. She hurried over to her dad and gave him a quick hug. "Thanks for bring-ing them in, Dad!" Ellie said. Then she turned to the class. "Surprise, everybody! Mrs. Wise said I could bring in a birthday treat!"

Sophie and the other students cheered.

Ellie's dad started passing out the cupcakes. Sophie sniffed at hers. Yum! Cinnamon hazelnut!

Ellie walked around too, placing a card on each student's desk.

Sophie glanced down. It was an invitation!

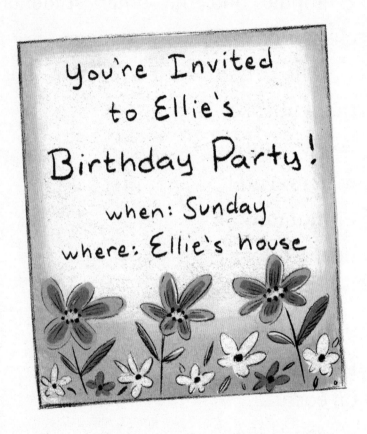

You're Invited to Ellie's Birthday Party!
when: Sunday
where: Ellie's house

"Sunday is my actual birthday," Ellie explained. "I hope all of you can come to my party."

Sophie wiggled happily in her seat.

Forget the math quiz, she told herself. *It's party time!*

— Chapter 2 —

The Shopping Trip

The next morning Sophie gobbled down her breakfast.

She loved her dad's special Saturday morning waffles. But she loved birthday parties even more. And after breakfast, Sophie and Winston were going to walk into town to shop for Ellie's present.

"Ready, Winston?" Sophie asked

impatiently. She couldn't help it!

Sophie grabbed Winston by the hand and led him toward the front door. Winston hopped along on one foot, still pulling on his shoe.

On their way down the path to town, Sophie and Winston made their shopping plan.

"I'd like to look in the Little Leaf Bookstore and the General Store," Sophie said.

Winston nodded. "Can we look in Handy's Hardware too?" he asked.

Sophie smiled and agreed. It didn't seem like the place to find a gift for Ellie. But Winston loved poking around in there.

The bell on the door jingled as the mice stepped into the bookstore. Winston hurried off to the easy-to-read shelf. Sophie browsed the new arrivals for young readers.

There were a few that looked great to her, including a how-to on pressing wildflowers and a new graphic novel with a mouse heroine.

But Sophie soon realized she didn't
know what kinds of books *Ellie* liked
best. Or what she already had.

Winston wound up buying a book
of mazes for himself. Then Sophie

and Winston headed off to the General Store.

There were lots of choices here: soaps, candy, socks, and playing cards. There was even a small toy

section. Sophie searched the shelves. Would Ellie like a yo-yo? A rubber stamp kit? A new jump rope?

Winston decided to get Ellie a shadow puppet kit that came with a pocket flashlight.

But nothing jumped out at Sophie.

They moved on to Handy's Hardware. Sophie was feeling discouraged. They'd already been to the two shops where they were most likely to find a gift. Sophie followed Winston up and down the aisles. He looked at shiny tools and peeked in drawers filled with nails. But Sophie's mind was already on where they could go next. Where else could she find something for Ellie?

Sophie came to the end of an aisle, stopped, and stared.

There, on a display table, was the most beautiful miniature house Sophie had ever seen!

The walls were made of wood. The roof shingles were squares of bark. The house stood propped open like a book. Sophie peeked inside.

The lower level was divided into two large rooms and a center hallway. The upper level had three bedrooms, each with different types of wallpaper. A wooden ladder connected the two floors.

The rooms were empty. But right away, Sophie's imagination started filling them with tiny tables, chairs, sofas, and rugs.

A sign on the table read:

It also included a sticker with the price. Whoa! The house was way too expensive a gift for Sophie to buy for Ellie.

But the thing was . . . Sophie didn't want to give it to *Ellie*.

Sophie wanted the house for herself.

— Chapter 3 —

Think Sparkly Thoughts

Sophie didn't find a gift for Ellie in town. But she did find inspiration. Mr. Handy's handcrafted miniature house had reminded her of something: Handmade things are special.

Instead of buying a gift, Sophie was going to *paint* one.

Back at home, she went upstairs to her room. She looked over her

painting supplies. Sophie had a bunch of standard colors. But a birthday painting called for special birthday paint.

Sophie wanted something eye-catching. Something festive. Something . . . *glittery!*

So that afternoon, Sophie was on a mission. She had once seen shimmery rocks down by the stream.

Maybe she could scrape off some flecks and grind them into a powder. Then she could add it to different colors to make glitter paint.

Sophie stopped by Hattie's house and asked if she wanted to help.

"Sure!" Hattie exclaimed. "I think I know where we can look."

The two friends headed upstream. As Hattie led the way, they talked about Ellie's party. Hattie had her gift all wrapped and ready. "I remembered she likes to knit," Hattie said.

"So I got her some colorful yarn."

"Great idea!" Sophie replied.

She told Hattie about her shopping trip that morning. "I didn't find anything for Ellie," Sophie said. "But I did see something amazing that *I* want to get someday." She described the house Mr. Handy had made. "It's like a miniature mouse house!"

Hattie frowned. "Couldn't it be a miniature *frog* house?" she asked.

Sophie shrugged. "I guess."

They passed some tall reeds. Sophie picked one, then tore it into smaller pieces. She b u n d l e d the pieces together to form a tiny brush.

She showed it to Hattie. "Look!"
Sophie said. "A little broom for the
mouse house!"

Hattie laughed.

They walked a little farther. Sophie
pointed out a teeny-tiny mushroom
growing in some moss. "That could
be a footstool in the mouse house!"
she cried. "What do you think?"

Hattie laughed. "I think you really, really want that mouse house!" she said.

Sophie laughed too. "Yeah," she admitted.

Hattie led Sophie to a spot where some rocks were half-buried in sand in the shallow water.

"Here!" Hattie said. She scooped up a handful of pebbles and rinsed them in the water. She held her hand out for Sophie to see.

The rocks sparkled in the sunlight.

"Wow!" Sophie exclaimed. "These are great!"

She picked out the most sparkly ones she could find. Then she took them home to grind them down. They were going to be perfect for making a glittery birthday painting for Ellie.

Chapter 4

The Mystery Gift

The next day, at the party, Sophie and Winston ran to greet Ellie. "Happy birthday!" they cried, and handed her their gifts.

Winston had put his in a striped gift bag. Sophie had rolled hers into a scroll, wrapped it in fabric, and tied it with a ribbon.

"Thank you so much!" Ellie

exclaimed, placing the items on a table.

As she did, one of the other gifts caught Sophie's eye. It was a very large box wrapped in fancy paper. On top was a big red bow.

Who had gotten Ellie such a big present? And what was inside?

Sophie felt a pang of doubt. Was her painting a good enough gift? She was proud of the way it had turned out. She just hoped Ellie would like it too.

It's the thought that counts, Sophie reminded herself. *Isn't it?* Besides, the other gifts on the table looked about the same size as hers and Winston's.

Sophie shook it off as the party got started. Ellie and her parents had created an acorn hunt. They had buried acorns all around their family's tree house.

"If you dig up an acorn with a gold-painted cap, you win a prize," Ellie explained.

Sophie and Winston did well. After all, mice have very good senses of smell. Sophie found three acorns and Winston found two—one with a gold cap!

Afterward, they played rounds of freeze tag, leapfrog, and red light, green light.

All that running around made everyone hungry. Soon they were

ready for Ellie's chocolate-nut birth-day cake.

Her mom and dad lit the candles on top. Ellie closed her eyes, made a wish, and blew them out—all in one breath!

"Hooray!" everyone cheered.

Finally, it was time for Ellie to open her gifts.

She opened Willy's first.  It was a set of colored pencils in a pretty tin that included erasers in many different shapes.

"I saw that your school pencils are all pretty short," Willy explained. "I thought you could use some new ones."

"I could!" Ellie agreed. "Thanks, Willy!"

Ben and James had gotten her one gift from both of them. "A puzzle!"

Ellie cried as she opened the box. "Oooh, this looks hard—but in a good way!"

Ellie also seemed to love the yarn Hattie had picked out. Hattie's sister, Lydie, went along with the theme and gave Ellie a new set of knitting needles.

Ellie laughed at Piper's gift: a tote bag with a smiling acorn that said I'M A NUT!

Next was a chess set from Owen, a polka-dot umbrella from Zoe, a card game from Malcolm, and then the shadow puppet kit from Winston. Ellie beamed with delight as she opened each one.

Sophie watched as Ellie reached for her present next. Ellie unwrapped the fabric, unfurled the painting, and gasped. "Sophie! Did *you* paint this?"

Sophie nodded.

"It's beautiful!" Ellie exclaimed. "Look!" She held the painting up so everyone could see. "How did you get it to shine like this?"

Sophie smiled proudly and then explained how she'd made the paint. Ellie looked very impressed. She really seemed to like it. Sophie felt so happy. And relieved!

Now there was only one gift

left—the big one. Ellie's mom picked it up and put it in front of Ellie. "This one is from your dad and me," said Mrs. Squirrel.

Aha! thought Sophie. That made sense.

Ellie peeled off a strip of paper. Now one corner of the gift was poking out. "What in the world?" Ellie said, confused by what she saw.

But to Sophie, the squares of bark looked strangely familiar.

She gasped. She knew that roof!

She knew it because it was the roof of the mouse house!

~ Chapter 5 ~

The Squirrel
House

Ellie unwrapped the rest of the gift. All the party guests crowded around Ellie to get a good look at the miniature house.

"Oh my gosh!" Ellie exclaimed. "Mom and Dad! I love it!" She jumped up and gave them a big hug. "Thank you so much!"

"It's so detailed!" Zoe said,

peeking inside the house. "Look at the wallpapers!"

"The window shutters open and close!" Owen said.

"Aw, it even comes with a little squirrel family," Lydie pointed out.

Sophie craned her neck to see. Sure enough, there in the downstairs hallway was a set of miniature squirrel dolls.

Next to Sophie, James leaned toward Winston. "Have you ever seen

anything like that?" James asked him. Winston nodded. "Yeah!" he blurted out. "We saw it in Handy's Hardware!" He turned to look at Sophie. "Didn't we?"

Sophie forced a smile and nodded.

"Isn't Mr. Handy talented?" asked Mr. Squirrel. "It's all handcrafted!"

"Yes," Sophie said, "it's truly one-of-a-kind." *And now it belongs to Ellie,* she thought.

Sophie tried very hard to hide her disappointment. She knew she was being silly. How had she gotten so attached to that house—in only one day?

Sophie sighed, put on a smile, and reached for a squirrel doll. "Can I be the little sister?" she asked Ellie.

Sophie figured if she couldn't own the house, at least she should take this chance to play with it.

Ellie nodded. "Of course!"

Back at home, Mrs. Mouse greeted Sophie and Winston. "How was the party?" she asked.

Sophie shrugged. "It was okay, I guess," she replied glumly. She flopped onto the sofa.

"Okay?" Winston cried in disbelief. "It was so fun! We played tons of games. Ellie's cake was yummy. And

I won this!" He held up the wooden car he got as a prize for the acorn hunt.

Winston drove it on the kitchen counter and up the stairs. Sophie heard him drive it down the hall to his room.

Mrs. Mouse came over and sat next to Sophie. "Did you and Winston go to the same party?" she asked with a smile.

Sophie shrugged and looked down. Feeling a little embarrassed, she told her mom about the mouse house—how she'd seen it the day before, and how Ellie's parents had bought it for Ellie.

"The party *was* fun," Sophie admitted. "I was just kind of . . . jealous, I guess."

It felt good to get her feelings out.

And Sophie's mom said just what Sophie needed. Nothing. Mrs. Mouse simply listened. Then she wrapped Sophie in a big, warm hug.

— Chapter 6—

Sophie on Edge

Sophie got her math quiz back on Monday morning. Mrs. Wise had made four big red circles around the problems Sophie had gotten wrong.

Sophie tugged at her whiskers as she looked it over. She had made some silly mistakes. On one problem, she added instead of subtracting. And her answers to the last three problems—the ones she had rushed through—were all wrong.

At lunchtime, Sophie went to get her lunch from her cubby. Owen hurried over with his quiz paper.

"I got a hundred!" Owen said excitedly. "How did you do?"

"I don't want to talk about it," she said grumpily.

Sophie dug around in her cubby. "Oh no," she moaned. "I left my lunch at home."

Hattie overheard Sophie. "You can have half of my sandwich," she told Sophie.

Sophie managed a smile. "Thanks, Hattie." It was nice of her. But Sophie had made herself a good

 sandwich that morning: apple slices, honey, and peanut butter on a cranberry scone. It bugged her to imagine it sitting at home.

"Okay, class," Mrs. Wise said after lunch. "Let's go over our new spelling words before we head outside for recess."

The students made their way to their desks. As Sophie sat down, Ellie waved at her from across the room. Ellie said something. But Sophie couldn't hear her.

What? Sophie mouthed back with a shrug.

It was time to stop talking. The room had quieted down. Mrs. Wise had her back to the class and was writing words on the chalkboard.

- Dandelion
- Tulip
- Parsnip
- R

Sophie saw Ellie take out a piece of paper. Ellie scribbled something on it and folded it up into a small square.

Ellie passed it to Piper at the desk next to her. Piper passed it to Owen.

Owen passed it behind him to Hattie.

Hattie passed it to Sophie.

Sophie unfolded the note and read:

You're such a great artist, Sophie! Thanks for the painting!

Sophie looked up. She smiled at Ellie. Then she picked up her pencil. Under Ellie's words, Sophie wrote back:

Sophie folded the note back up. "Pssst, Hattie!" she said, holding it out.

But Hattie didn't move. And she seemed kind of nervous, Sophie noticed.

Sophie followed Hattie's gaze. Up at the front of the room, Mrs. Wise was looking right at Sophie.

"And what's that, Sophie?" Mrs. Wise asked sternly. "Something more important than spelling words?"

Sophie opened her mouth to answer. But no words came out.

"Please put it away," Mrs. Wise added.

Sophie shoved the note inside her desk. Mrs. Wise went on with her lesson. Sophie tried to focus on the spelling words. But she couldn't concentrate. She was so embarrassed, she wished she could melt into her chair.

Finally, Mrs. Wise dismissed everyone to go out to recess. Sophie slinked out the door with her head down.

Outside on the playground, Ellie ran over.

"I'm so sorry, Sophie," Ellie said with a nervous giggle. "I didn't mean to get you in trouble."

Something about Ellie's giggle set Sophie off.

"I'm glad you can laugh about it," Sophie snapped. "*You're* not the one who got yelled at!"

Ellie's face fell. "Oh, no. Sophie, I wasn't laughing at you—"

"Just don't pass me notes in class ever again," Sophie interrupted. She walked off to swing on the swings by herself.

creative sparks

That night Sophie tossed and turned in her bed. She'd been trying to fall asleep for a long time. But every time she started to drift off, she remembered what she had said to Ellie.

Just don't pass me notes in class ever again.

Sophie covered her head with her pillow. Ellie had been trying to

apologize. "Why did I get so upset?" Sophie asked herself.

She knew the answer. She had been in a bad mood. She'd gotten so many problems wrong on the quiz. She'd forgotten her lunch. Then she'd been scolded in front of the whole class.

But there
was one more
thing, too.

Sophie took
it out on Ellie
because Ellie
had the mouse
house. *I'm the
one who should
say sorry to her*, Sophie decided.

The next morning, when Sophie
got to school, she walked right up
to Ellie.

"I'm sorry I got so mad yesterday,"
Sophie said. "I was just . . . having a

bad day." She left out the part about feeling jealous.

Ellie smiled. "That's okay, Sophie. I understand. It wasn't fair that you got in trouble and I didn't."

Sophie breathed a sigh of relief. She felt so much better.

"Hey," Ellie went on, "do you want to maybe come over and play this weekend? My new squirrel house could really use some furniture. And you're so artistic!" Ellie clasped her hands together pleadingly. "Maybe you could help me make a few things?"

Sophie was caught off guard. "Oh! Uh . . . um . . . ," she stammered. She was racking her brain for an excuse to  say no. But her mind was a total blank.

"Okay!" Sophie blurted out. "Sure!"

Sophie forced herself to stop in at Handy's Hardware on the way home.

Why couldn't I think of an excuse? she thought. *Do I want to make furniture for Ellie's squirrel house? No! I want to make it for*

my own mouse house!

But Sophie had agreed. And now she felt like she needed to help Ellie— at least a little bit.

I'll help her make one thing, Sophie decided. *Just one!*

She browsed through the hardware store. She looked for ideas in the plumbing section. She rummaged in the wood scrap bin. She looked at doorknobs, locks, fasteners, and tools.

On one shelf, she spotted spools of twine. Sophie picked one up.

Sitting on end, this spool would make the perfect tiny table, she thought. *And smaller ones—like thread spools—could be a set of matching stools.*

Sophie smiled. The ideas started coming, one after another.

Maybe she would make a few more things, after all. Just a few more.

Chapter 8

Think Small

For the rest of the week Sophie made all kinds of teeny-tiny furniture.

So she didn't have a mouse house to put them in. It was still a fun way to use her imagination!

On Tuesday, Sophie stopped in at Mrs. Weaver's shop, In Stitches. Mrs. Weaver was the town seamstress. Sophie told her about her

new hobby making tiny furniture.

"Well, you're welcome to take anything you like from my fabric scraps," Mrs. Weaver said kindly.

Sophie clapped her hands. "Thank you! That would be perfect!" she replied.

Sophie didn't need big pieces. Tiny sofas and pillows could be made from tiny pieces of fabric.

Sophie picked up a piece of ribbon. It was the perfect size for a tiny tablecloth.

Mrs. Weaver also gave Sophie six empty thread spools for the stools she had in mind. Then she pulled some buttons from her sewing box.

"Can you use these?" Mrs. Weaver asked.

Sophie studied them. "Yes!" she replied. They looked like miniature dishes.

On Wednesday, Sophie stopped in at the General Store.

She picked up a small wooden soap dish. "A bed!" she exclaimed.

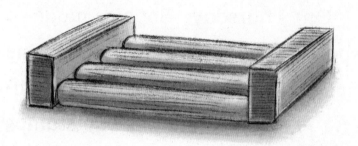

All it needed was a handkerchief for a bedspread and some tiny pillows.

In the food aisle Sophie stopped in front of the canned goods. The can of creamed corn had such a colorful label. If she peeled it off, could it be wall art?

Hmm, maybe too big, Sophie decided. But it gave her another idea. Postage stamps!

On Thursday, Sophie made a special trip to the post office. She  picked out three different postage stamps with pretty designs. They really were tiny works of art!

After school on Friday, Sophie worked on putting all her tiny creations together. When she was done, she had made enough furniture for a miniature dining room . . .

. . . and a miniature bedroom.

"Wow!" cried Winston, peeking into Sophie's room. "You *made* all of that?"

Sophie smiled and nodded. She felt very proud of her work.

"I can't wait to see it all in Ellie's miniature house!" Sophie said.

Wait. What? Sophie thought.

She was suddenly surprised by her own words. But it was true. She'd had so much fun making the furniture. She had almost forgotten that she didn't have a mouse house to put it in.

Sophie sighed.

The truth was, it seemed like Ellie's squirrel house was where the furniture was meant to be.

Chapter 9

Squirrel Housewarming

"Sophie!" Ellie called down from her family's tree house. "Come on up!"

A ladder led up to Ellie's front door. Sophie scrambled up, carrying a box under one arm.

This was only Sophie's second time inside Ellie's tree house. And at the birthday party, she hadn't really looked around. Now Sophie saw that

the home had four floors, all connected by ladders. Ellie led Sophie up
to her room on the top floor. Instead
of a bed, Ellie had a hammock. From
her window, she had a beautiful view
of the forest below.

And there, on Ellie's rug, was the
squirrel house.

It was just as perfect as Sophie
remembered. But it was still empty.
Ellie's squirrel dolls lay on the floor,
since there were no chairs or beds
for them.

Sophie held out the box in her
hands. "I brought you something,"

she told Ellie. "Open it!"

Ellie looked surprised. She lifted the lid and gasped.

Inside were all of the miniature items Sophie had made.

"What is all this?" Ellie asked in awe. Very gently, she started taking the furniture out of the box, piece by piece. "These are amazing. Where did they come from?"

Sophie smiled. "I made them!" she said.

Ellie's mouth dropped open in surprise. "Sophie!" she said. "When I asked for your help to make a few things, I didn't

mean you had to do all this! All by
yourself?" She studied the postage-
stamp art that Sophie had made
teeny-tiny frames for. "You must
have spent so much time on this!"

Sophie nodded. "I did. But it was
fun," she told Ellie. "And now I can't
wait to see how they look in your
house!"

Together, Sophie and Ellie arranged
all the items. Then they played with
the squirrel dolls in the newly fur-
nished rooms. The bed was just the
right size for a squirrel to nap on. And
there were enough stools for each

member of the family at dinnertime.

Sophie and Ellie played with the squirrel house all afternoon.

Then it was time for Sophie to go. But first, there was something she wanted to say.

"Ellie," she said, "you know how I
saw this house at Handy's Hardware?
I . . . well . . . I really wanted it for
myself."

"You did?" Ellie said.

Sophie nodded. "So when you got it, I felt jealous. It's another reason I got so mad at you on Monday." She looked sheepishly at her feet. "I'm sorry. *Again*."

This one felt like a more honest apology.

"Oh, that's okay Sophie," Ellie replied gently. "Gosh. Now I wish Mr. Handy had made two of them, so you could have one too."

Sophie laughed. "That would be so great!"

Ellie invited Sophie to come over and play with the squirrel house any

time she wanted. Sophie agreed she
would.

"Next time I'll show you how
I made the dresser," Sophie said.
"Maybe we can make one for the
other bedroom."

Sophie skipped home happily, thinking about more tiny furniture ideas.

When she got there, she told her parents about her afternoon. "We played with Ellie's squirrel house the whole time. I made her a bunch of furniture for it."

Mrs. Mouse put an arm around Sophie's shoulder. "Wow, I'm very impressed," she said. "I know how much you wanted that house. It was so nice of you to help Ellie decorate it."

Mr. Mouse was sketching in his design notebook. He was an architect, so he often had a pencil in his hand—and usually one tucked behind his ear, too. He stopped sketching and looked up at Sophie. "I agree," he said. "I'm proud of you, Sophie. I just hope you're ready to make some *more* tiny house furniture."

Sophie looked confused. "What for, Dad?"

Mr. and Mrs. Mouse smiled mischievously. "For this!" Mr. Mouse replied. He flipped his sketchbook around.

There on the page was a design for a beautiful Victorian-style dollhouse. It looked . . . like a mouse house!

"What do you say we build this together?" Mr. Mouse said.

Sophie gasped. "Really?" she cried.

Mr. Mouse nodded. "I do know a *little* something about building."

Sophie jumped up and down gleefully. "And I know a little something about tiny furniture!"

She couldn't wait to get started.

The End

You'll also enjoy

"Ready or not, here I come!" Sophie shouted.

She opened her eyes and looked around. Owen and Hattie were gone. The three friends were playing hide-and-seek by Owen's house. Sophie was the seeker.

She listened for a rustle of leaves

or a snap of a twig. She sniffed the air. Really, though, she didn't need any clues. There were only two good hiding places in Owen's yard.

First, Sophie checked inside the hollow log. It was a tight squeeze for Hattie or herself, but Owen fit easily. Sophie peered inside. "Found you!" she cried.

Owen wriggled out. "Aww," he moaned. "That was quick."

Next Sophie scurried over to a baby fir tree. Hattie was pretty well cam-ouflaged by the needles. But Sophie could see her shoes.

the adventures of
SOPHIE MOUS[E]

For excerpts, activities, and more ab[out]
these adorable tales & tails, visi[t]
AdventuresofSophieMouse.com!